This *LADYBIRD TALE*
belongs to

....

Puss in Boots

Retold by Vera Southgate M.A., B.COM
with illustrations by Daniel Howarth

LADYBIRD 🐞 TALES

ONCE UPON A TIME there was a miller who had three sons. He was so poor that when he died he left nothing but his mill, his donkey and his cat.

The mill, of course, had to be left to his eldest son. The donkey went to his second son. Then all that was left for the youngest son was his father's cat.

"Alas!" sighed the youngest son, "Puss is no use to me and I am too poor even to feed him."

"Do not worry, dear master," said the cat. "Give me a pair of boots and a bag and you will find that we are not as badly off as you think."

The miller's son was very surprised to hear a cat talk. "A cat that can talk is perhaps clever enough to do as he promises," he thought to himself.

So, with his last few coins, the miller's son bought Puss a pair of boots and a bag.

Puss was delighted with the boots. He pulled them on and strutted up and down in front of his master. He looked so proud of himself that the miller's son could not help but laugh at him.

From that time onwards, the miller's son always called him Puss in Boots.

Then Puss slung the bag over his shoulder and went off to the garden. There he gathered some fresh lettuce leaves which he put in his bag.

Next, Puss in Boots set off across the fields. He stopped when he came to a rabbit hole. Then, leaving the mouth of his bag open, he lay quietly down nearby.

A plump rabbit soon peeped out of the hole. It smelled the fresh lettuce leaves and came nearer. They were too tempting. First the rabbit's nose went into the bag and then its head. Puss quickly pulled the strings and the rabbit was caught.

With the rabbit in his bag, Puss in Boots marched off to the palace and asked to see the king.

When he was brought before him, he made a low bow and said, "Your Majesty, please accept this rabbit as a gift from my lord, the Marquis of Carrabas."

The king was amused by this cat wearing boots and talking. "Tell your master," he said, "that I accept his gift and I am much obliged."

On another day, Puss again lay down, as if he were dead, in a field. Once more his bag was open beside him. This time he caught two fine partridges.

Again, Puss in Boots took his catch to the king. As before, the king accepted the gift from the Marquis of Carrabas. He was so pleased with the partridges that he ordered the cat to be taken to the royal kitchens and fed.

As it happened, the king had a daughter who was said to be the most beautiful princess in the world.

One day, Puss in Boots heard that the king and his daughter were going for a drive along by the river. Puss ran immediately to the miller's son and said, "My master, if you will now do as I tell you, your future will be made."

"What would you have me do?" asked the miller's son.

"Come with me, my master," replied Puss and led him to the bank of the river.

"There are only two things I want you to do," said the cat. "First, you must bathe here in the river. Secondly, you must believe that you are not yourself but the Marquis of Carrabas."

"I have never heard of the Marquis of Carrabas," said the miller's son, "but I will do as you say."

While the miller's son was bathing in the river, the royal carriages came into sight. The king was in his carriage with his daughter beside him. His nobles were riding behind.

Suddenly they were startled by a cry of "Help! Help! My lord the Marquis of Carrabas is drowning!"

The king, looking out of his carriage, could see no one but Puss in Boots who was running up and down beside the river. However, the king told his nobles to run quickly to help the drowning man.

Puss ran back to the king as soon as the nobles had dragged his master from the river. Making a low bow, he said, "Your Majesty, what shall my poor master do, for a thief has stolen his clothes?"

Now, the truth was that Puss in Boots had hidden the clothes under a large stone.

"That is most unfortunate," said the king. "We cannot leave him there without clothes." So he gave orders to a servant to fetch a suit from the palace.

When the miller's son was dressed in a suit of good clothes, he looked a very fine man indeed.

The king then invited him to go for a drive with them. So the miller's son sat in the carriage beside the princess.

Puss ran on quickly, ahead of the carriage. He stopped when he reached a meadow where the mowers were cutting the grass.

Puss spoke to the mowers. "The king is coming this way and he may ask you whose meadow this is. Unless you say that it belongs to the Marquis of Carrabas, you shall all be chopped as fine as mincemeat."

The mowers were simple fellows and they were terrified to hear a cat talking in such a fierce voice.

A few minutes later, the king and his nobles drove by. As the king passed the large, lovely meadow, he stopped his carriage and spoke to the mowers.

"Tell me," he asked, "who owns this fine meadow?"

"It belongs to the Marquis of Carrabas, your Majesty," replied the mowers.

At that, the king turned to the miller's son. "You do indeed own a fine meadow, my lord," he said.

Meanwhile, Puss had run further on along the road. He reached a cornfield in which reapers were busy cutting the corn.

"The king will soon drive by," said Puss to the reapers. "He might ask whose cornfields these are. Unless you say that they belong to the Marquis of Carrabas, you shall all be chopped as fine as mincemeat."

The reapers, just like the mowers, were terrified to hear a cat talking in such a fierce voice.

A few minutes later, the king and all his nobles came into sight. Once more the king stopped his carriage.

"Tell me," he said to the reapers, "who owns these cornfields?"

"They belong to the Marquis of Carrabas," replied the reapers.

"What a rich man he must be and how handsome he looks," said the king to himself. "I do believe he would make a good husband for my daughter."

Now the fields really belonged to an ogre and this ogre lived in a castle a little further along.

Puss in Boots hurried along the road until he reached the castle. Then he knocked on the door which was opened by the ogre himself.

"Sir," said Puss, "I am on a journey and, as I have often heard how wonderful you are, I have taken the liberty of calling to see you."

The ogre was startled to hear a cat talking. Yet he was pleased to learn that the cat had heard how wonderful he was. He immediately invited Puss into the castle.

"I have heard," said Puss, "that you can change yourself into any animal you choose."

"That is true," replied the ogre, and he instantly changed himself into a lion. Puss got a terrible fright. He quickly scrambled to the top of a very high dresser, out of harm's way.

At once the ogre changed himself from a lion back to an ogre again, whereupon Puss jumped down.

"Sir, I must tell you that you frightened me," said Puss. "Yet it must not be too difficult for such a big fellow as yourself to change into a large animal like a lion."

"It would be even more wonderful if a huge ogre could change himself into a tiny animal," went on Puss. "I suppose you could not, for instance, change yourself into a mouse?"

"Could not!" cried the ogre. "I can change myself into anything I choose. You shall see!" Immediately, he became a little grey mouse, which scampered across the floor in front of Puss in Boots.

With one spring, Puss pounced upon the mouse and gobbled it up. So there was an end to the ogre.

By this time the king's carriages were arriving at the castle. Puss in Boots, hearing the carriage wheels, ran to the gate. Bowing low, he said, "Welcome, your Majesty, to the castle of the Marquis of Carrabas."

"What, my lord," cried the king, turning to the miller's son, "does this castle also belong to you? I have nothing so grand in my whole kingdom."

The miller's son did not speak but gave his hand to the princess to help her from the carriage.

They all entered the castle where they found a wonderful feast ready to be served. It had been prepared for guests whom the ogre had expected. Fortunately, the ogre's friends did not arrive, as news had reached them that the king was in the castle.

The king and the princess, the nobles and the miller's son all sat down to the feast. Puss in Boots stood by the side of his master.

Every moment the king became more and more charmed with the miller's son. When the feast was over, the king said to him, "There is no one in the world I would rather have as my son-in-law. I now make you a prince."

Then the prince said that there was no one in the world he would like so much for his wife as the princess.

And the princess said there was no one in the world she would like so much for a husband as the prince.

So the two were married and lived happily ever after, in the ogre's castle.

Puss in Boots was very happy, living in the castle. He was always the greatest favourite with the king, the prince and the princess.

Never again had Puss to hunt for a meal. He lived on the fat of the land until the end of his days.

A History of Puss in Boots

The tale of *Puss in Boots* has inspired choreographers, composers and many other artists over the centuries. Most recently Puss appeared as a character in the hugely popular *Shrek* films. Following Puss's success in *Shrek,* this loveable feline went on to star in his own film, aptly named *Puss in Boots*!

The character of Puss in Boots that we know and love today is a male cat. But Puss was originally thought to be female in early oral interpretations of the story, such as in Basile's version included in his collection *Pentamarone*, published in 1634.

In most literary versions, Puss is male. French author Charles Perrault published *Puss in Boots* in his *Histoires ou Contes du Temps Passé* in 1697 under the title *Le Maître Chat ou le Chat Botté*.

Vera Southgate's 1967 Ladybird retelling boosted the popularity of this tale, making it a firm favourite for a new generation of children.

Collect more fantastic
LADYBIRD 🐞 TALES

Little Red Riding Hood

9781409311126

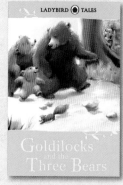

Goldilocks and the Three Bears

9781409311119

Cinderella

9781409311072

Jack and the Beanstalk

9781409311102

The Gingerbread Man

9781409311096

The Three Little Pigs

9781409311089

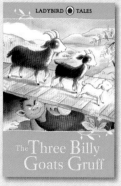

The Three Billy Goats Gruff

9781409311065

Hansel and Gretel

9781409311133

Puss in Boots

9781409311225

Rapunzel

9781409311195

Rumpelstiltskin

9781409311164

The Elves and the Shoemaker

9781409311188

Snow White and the Seven Dwarfs

9781409311171

The Enormous Turnip

9781409311218

The Magic Porridge Pot

9781409311201

Sleeping Beauty

9781409311157

Endpapers taken from series 606d,
first published in 1964

A catalogue record for this book is available from the British Library

Published by Ladybird Books Ltd
80 Strand London WC2R 0RL
A Penguin Company

002

© Ladybird Books Ltd MMXII

ISBN: 978-1-40931-122-5

Printed in China